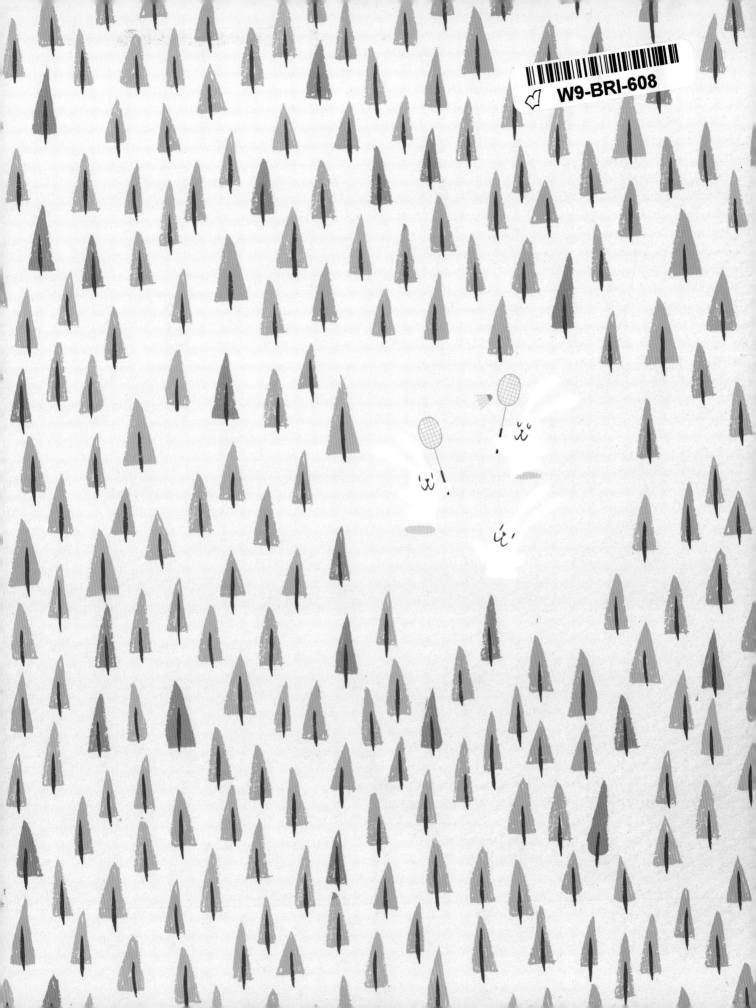

 **Don't make me come up there, mountain!**

BUDDY AND THE BUNNIES IN:

Don't PLAY with your PLAy food!

Bob Shea

Ɗisney • Hyperion Books / New York

Published by Disney • Hyperion Books,

an imprint of Disney Book Group.

No part of this book may be reproduced or

transmitted in any form or by any means,

electronic or mechanical, including

photocopying, recording, or by any information

storage and retrieval system, without

written permission from the publisher.

For information address

Disney•Hyperion Books,

125 West End Avenue,

New York, New York 10023.

First Edition

10 9 8 7 6 5 4 3 2 1

H106-9333-5-13258

Printed in Malaysia

Reinforced binding

Library of Congress Cataloging-in-Publication Data

Shea, Bob, author, illustrator.

Buddy and the bunnies in Don't play with your food! /

by Bob Shea.—First edition.

pages   cm

Summary: "A monster named Buddy is

determined to eat some cute little bunnies,

until they prove to be more enjoyable as

playmates"

ISBN 978-1-4231-6807-2 (hardback)

[1. Monsters—Fiction. 2. Rabbits—Fiction.

3. Friendship—Fiction. 4. Humorous stories.]

I. Title. II. Title: Don't play with your food.

PZ7.S53743Bu 2013

[E]—dc23   2013022015

Visit www.disneyhyperionbooks.com

FLOWERS? GROSS! P-U!

For Ryan

For Colleen

For Ryan and Colleen

Outta my way, trees!

DRY UP, LAKE!

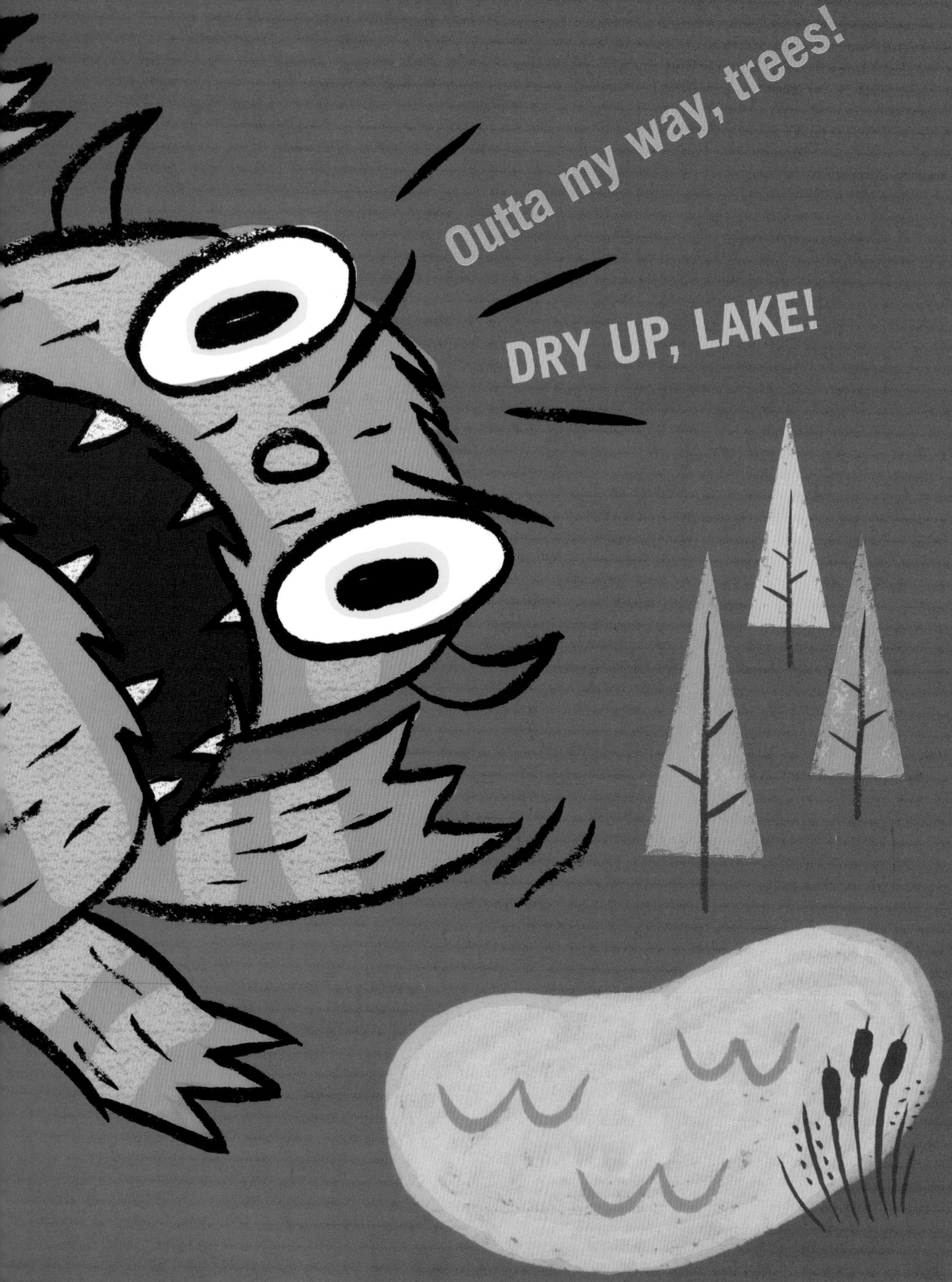

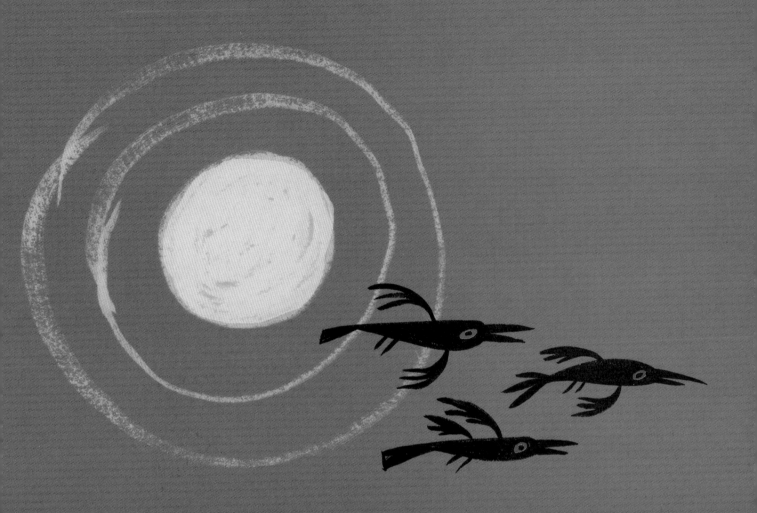

You're not so hot, SUN!

You better run, birds!

"Oh, no!" said the bunnies.

"No, please, no!
We were about to make cupcakes!"

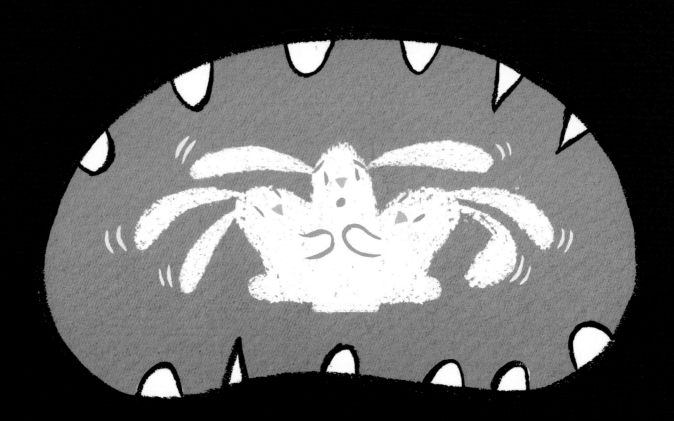

TEE HEE!

"What kind of monster do you think I am?" said Buddy.
"Cupcakes first.
Bunnies for dessert."

They played hide-and-seek while the cupcakes baked in the oven.

TEE HEE!

TEE HEE!

One, two, three . . .

DING!

"Be careful, Buddy.
The pan is very hot."

Each bunny had one cupcake. Buddy had five.
There were four cupcakes left.

Buddy ate them.

"Ugh, I'm so full.
Would you bunnies mind if
I ate you tomorrow?"

"Nice meeting you, Buddy!"
said the bunnies.

Buddy came back the next day.

"Hey, guys! Hop in my mouth so I can eat you!"

"It's too hot to be eaten," said the bunnies.
"Can we go swimming instead?"

"Hmmm . . . I don't know. . . ." said Buddy.

"Please! Please! Please!"

"How about I eat you, then I go swimming."

"Oh, no! You mustn't go swimming right after you eat!
 You'll get a cramp!"

"This is way more fun than a cramp!" said Buddy.

"If you bunnies are half as delicious as you are nice, I am in for a treat."

Buddy and the bunnies laughed and splashed all afternoon.

Swimming under the hot sun tuckered everyone out.
Buddy and the bunnies took a nap in the tall, cool grass.

When Buddy woke up, he thought,
I really should eat them,
but I hate to wake them.
They look so cute when they're napping.

Buddy patted the bunnies' heads and whispered,
"I promise to eat you tomorrow."

Then he tiptoed away.

Rahhhhh!

oh!

What the . . . ?

The next day Buddy couldn't believe his eyes. All the bunnies wore stripes just like his.

"Surprise!" yelled the bunnies.
"We started a Stripey-Stripe Club in your honor."

"That's so nice!" said Buddy, wiping away a tear.
"Now climb in my mouth so I can eat you!"

"Oh, no! First the club will have to vote on that!"
There was one vote for eating the bunnies.
There were seven votes for going to the carnival.

Seven?

They played all the games and rode all the rides.
The bunnies liked the spinny, whippy rides the best.

Not Buddy.

"Bad news, bunnies. I don't feel so good.
I don't think I'll be able to eat you today. . . ."

"We know, Buddy. See you tomorrow!"

The next day, Buddy said,

"Okay, no more fooling around. Today I'm going to eat you bunnies first thing."

"OH, NO!" said the bunnies.
"Didn't you like baking cupcakes with us?"

"Yeah, sure, that was fun," said Buddy.

"And didn't you like going swimming with us?"

"Yeah, that was a blast."

"Didn't you like going to the carnival with us?"

"Sure, until I got dizzy."

"Well, then you can't eat us."

"Why not?"

"Didn't your mom ever tell you?"

"Tell me what?"

"Don't play with your food!"

Sniff!

"You bunnies tricked me!" said Buddy.

"Oh, no!" said the bunnies.
"We wouldn't do that. We like you, Buddy."

"Now I feel terrible," said Buddy.
"After I eat you bunnies, I'll be all alone!
No Stripey-Stripe Club. No swimming.
No hide-and-seek . . .
Hey, weren't there seven of you yesterday?"

"**Wait a second . . .**
my food never makes me sad!
Maybe you are not my food at all!
Maybe you are my . . .

"And I'm pretty sure
you're not supposed to eat
your friends!"

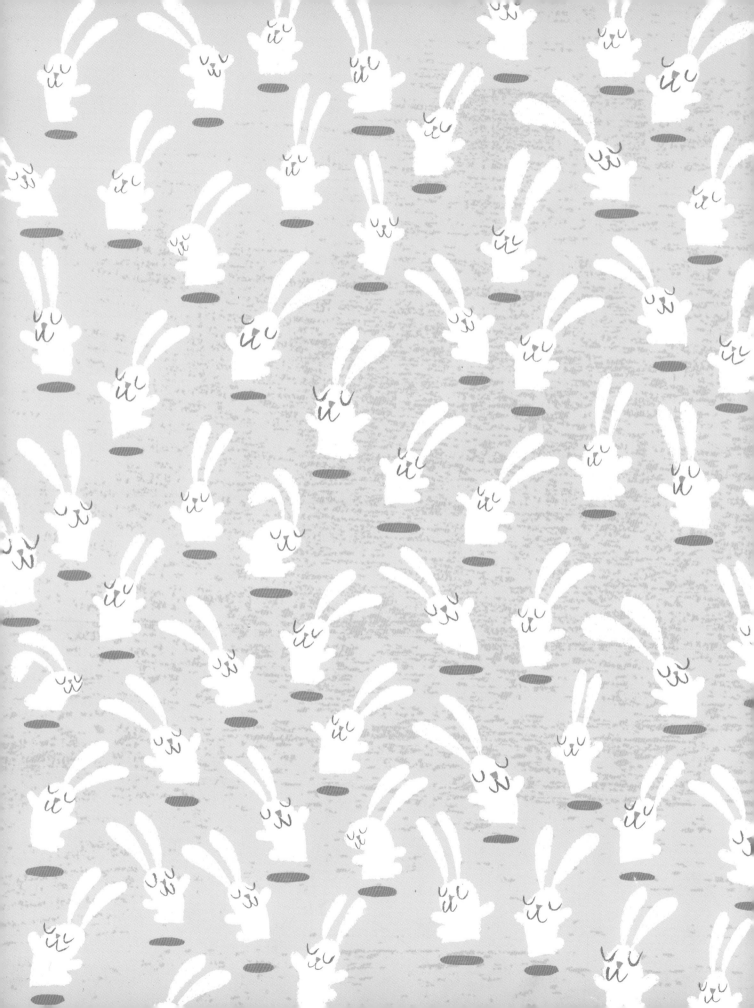